# ADVENTURE ANNIE GOES TO WORK

by
**Toni Buzzeo**

illustrated by
**Amy Wummer**

DIAL BOOKS FOR YOUNG READERS

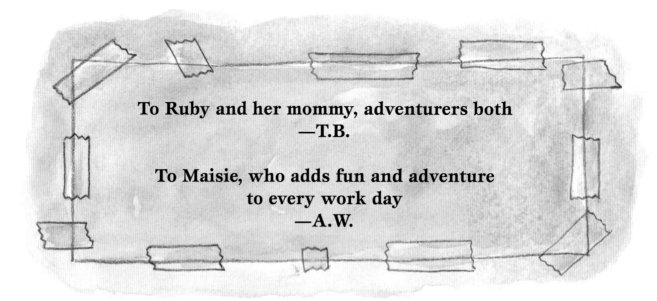

**To Ruby and her mommy, adventurers both**
**—T.B.**

**To Maisie, who adds fun and adventure**
**to every work day**
**—A.W.**

DIAL BOOKS FOR YOUNG READERS
A division of Penguin Young Readers Group
Published by The Penguin Group
Penguin Group (USA) Inc., 375 Hudson Street, New York, NY 10014, U.S.A.
Penguin Group (Canada), 90 Eglinton Avenue East, Suite 700,
Toronto, Ontario, Canada M4P 2Y3 (a division of Pearson Penguin Canada Inc.)
Penguin Books Ltd, 80 Strand, London WC2R 0RL, England
Penguin Ireland, 25 St. Stephen's Green, Dublin 2, Ireland (a division of Penguin Books Ltd)
Penguin Group (Australia), 250 Camberwell Road, Camberwell,
Victoria 3124, Australia (a division of Pearson Australia Group Pty Ltd)
Penguin Books India Pvt Ltd, 11 Community Centre, Panchsheel Park, New Delhi - 110 017, India
Penguin Group (NZ), 67 Apollo Drive, Rosedale, North Shore 0632, New Zealand (a division of Pearson New Zealand Ltd)
Penguin Books (South Africa) (Pty) Ltd, 24 Sturdee Avenue, Rosebank, Johannesburg 2196, South Africa
Penguin Books Ltd, Registered Offices: 80 Strand, London WC2R 0RL, England

Designed by Jasmin Rubero
Text set in ITC Esprit
Manufactured in China on acid-free paper
1 3 5 7 9 10 8 6 4 2

Library of Congress Cataloging-in-Publication Data
Buzzeo, Toni.
Adventure Annie goes to work / by Toni Buzzeo ; illustrated by Amy Wummer.
p.   cm.
Summary: When she goes to work with her mother on a Saturday,
Adventure Annie uses her own special methods to help find a missing report
ISBN 978-0-8037-3233-9
[1. Mothers and daughters—Fiction. 2. Lost and found possessions—Fiction.] I. Wummer, Amy, ill. II. Title.
PZ7.B9832Ad 2009
[E]—dc22
2008007679

*The illustrations were prepared using pencil and watercolor on Strathmore Bristol paper.*

"Wake up, Adventure Annie,"
Mommy calls from the door.

I rise. Morning shines.
It's Adventure Annie Saturday.
I grab my adventure cape
and squizzle into my sparkle tights.

The telephone rings.
I zip to the kitchen.

"Will I have a
mountaintop
adventure?"
"Not today,"
says Mommy.
She squeezes the
phone to her ear.

"Will I have a deep,
dark jungle adventure?"
"Maybe tomorrow," says Mommy.
She touches her finger to her lips.

"What adventure? What adventure?"
"You'll see," Mommy whispers.
I tap tap tap my toes.

"Let's go," I say.

　Mommy leans her head on the fridge.

"I'm sorry, Annie Grace. We can't play today.

　The big report is missing and I have to go to work."

"But it's Adventure Annie Saturday!"
"I know," Mommy says.
"Hey, how about a Big Report
Treasure Hunt?"
I give her the
Adventure Annie thumbs-up.

"Adventure Annie to the rescue,"
I sing.
We hop to it.

I whirl through spinning doors,
dragging Mommy by the hand.

The elevator ding-dings
and swallows us inside.

I poke every button twice.
We zoom and stop,
    zoom and stop,
        zoom and stop, stop, stop.

At the coatrack Mommy reaches for my cape.
"No, no!" I say. "Adventure Annie needs her cape
for hunting treasure."
"I have a better idea," Mommy says.

She rolls a chair up close to her desk.

She hands me paper and pencils and tape.

"You work while I go hunting down the hall."

But office work isn't Adventure Annie work.

Treasure hunting is!
I sneak out the door
and tiptoe in the other direction.

On TV when something is lost,
   adventurers check their maps.
      I will need a map for checking too.
         I jiggle doorknobs down the hall,

one—

two—

three,

until a door swings open wide. Map supplies!

I climb up high

and duck down low.

I fill my pockets full.

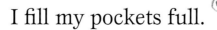

I ziggle up and down the halls.

I zaggle round corners
and under chairs.

I sneak,

I peek,

I explore.

When I know my directions
from here to there,
from there to here,
I draw the map that's in my mind.

Then I poke my nose into Mommy's office.
She's back behind her desk.
"What color is the report, Mommy?" I ask.

"It's in a gold folder," she says.
"And what are you doing in the hall?"
"Oopsie," I say.

When Mommy's bottom is in the air,

I slip back out the door.

I follow the arrow on my map
that points to a climbing mountain.

I dig my feet in tight
    and snatch up
    handfuls of gold.

My treasure teeters
    and totters
    as I carry it
    down the hall.

I trip through Mommy's office door.
"Is it one of these?" I ask.
"Goodness no!" she says.

She points me to my seat.

"When is the last time you saw it?"
   I whisper.
"I sent it to that jungle of a copy room
   yesterday afternoon."
   She frowns.
"But I didn't see it there
   just now."

Mommy pokes her head
into the cabinet,
and I duck out
one more time.

I *know* my map can help.

I follow the squiggle this time
and creep toward the deepest jungle.

Branches reach down
and I jump to catch hold.
Uh-oh.

I crawl through the dirt

and the dark and the deep,
    searching for the lost treasure.

Then daylight shines in.
"Oh NO!" Mommy cries.
"Oh YES!" I hop up.
I pull the treasure from inside my cape.

"That's it!" Mommy shouts.
   She gives me the Adventure Annie thumbs-up
   and together we sing,

## "Adventure Annie to the rescue!"